For Gus, Bronson, Linus, George,
and Frankie – superheroes all

S. H. and D. H.

To Ninja Princesses Isla and Nova

L. P.

THE *Princess* IN **BLACK**

TAKES A HOLIDAY

Shannon Hale & Dean Hale

illustrated by
LeUyen Pham

WALKER
BOOKS

First published in Great Britain 2018 by Walker Books Ltd
87 Vauxhall Walk, London SE11 5HJ

2 4 6 8 10 9 7 5 3 1

Text © 2016 Shannon and Dean Hale
Illustrations © 2016 LeUyen Pham

The right of Shannon and Dean Hale, and LeUyen Pham to be identified as
authors/illustrator of this work has been asserted by them in accordance with
the Copyright, Designs and Patents Act 1988

This book has been typeset in Kennerly

Printed in China

British Library Cataloguing in Publication Data:
a catalogue record for this book is available from the British Library

ISBN 978-1-4063-8003-3

www.walker.co.uk

Chapter 1

It was dawn. The Princess in Black had battled monsters all night. And so Princess Magnolia was tired.

Princess Magnolia lay down in her fluffy princess bed. She closed her eyes. She was almost asleep when...

"The monster alarm," she muttered.
"Not again."

She stumbled into the broom closet. She slipped off her frilly pyjamas. She fell into her black costume. Now she was the Princess in Black.

A very sleepy Princess in Black.

She went down the secret chute.

Onto the back of her pony, Blacky.

And into the goat pasture. Just as she had fourteen other times that week. "ROAR!" said a toothy monster.

"Did you say 'snore'?" asked the Princess in Black.

The toothy monster shook its head. "NO. ROAR."

The Princess in Black wished it had said "snore." She wished she were snoring right then.

"EAT GOATS!" said the monster.

"They're not your goats," the Princess in Black mumbled. "They're Duff's goats. Go back to Monster Land."

The toothy monster did not want to go back to Monster Land. The toothy monster was quite set on eating goats.

So the toothy monster and the
Princess in Black waged battle.

DOUBLE DOZY

DOOZY FLING!

The monster picked up the Princess in Black in its fist. It opened its toothy mouth. It roared again.

The Princess in Black opened her mouth. She didn't roar back. She yawned.

Just then, someone pulled the monster's tail.

Chapter 2

A boy in a mask and cape pulled the monster's tail. A boy the Princess in Black had never seen before.

"Who are you?" asked the Princess in Black. "And where is Duff the goat boy?"

"I am the Goat Avenger!" said the Goat Avenger. "And Duff the goat boy is busy. Somewhere else. Not here."

same ------->

same

The Goat Avenger was the same height as her friend, Duff. He even had the same smile. But it couldn't be Duff. Duff did not wear a mask.

same

same

"That's funny," said the Princess in Black. "Duff the goat boy is always here. This is his goat pasture. These are his goats."

"EAT GOATS!" said the monster.

The monster was still holding the Princess in Black. The monster still had a lot of teeth.

"YOU MAY NOT EAT THE GOATS!" said the Princess in Black and the Goat Avenger.

The monster winced. There were too many people with masks. It was all very confusing.

The monster put down the Princess in Black. It stuffed itself back into the hole. In Monster Land, no one wore masks.

Chapter 3

"That was the fifteenth monster this week," said the Princess in Black.

She yawned again. She curled up on the grass. Blacky snuggled up beside her.

"You look tired," said the Goat Avenger.

The Princess in Black closed her eyes. A goat licked her ear. She rolled over. Another goat nibbled her hair.

"You need a holiday," said the Goat Avenger.

The Princess in Black opened one eye.

"What's a holiday?" she asked.

"You take a break from work," he said. "You go somewhere nice. You rest."

"That sounds amazing. But I can't take a holiday. Who will protect the goats?"

The Goat Avenger put his fist on his hip.

"Never fear," he said. "The Goat Avenger is here!"

Chapter 4

"A holiday," said the Princess in Black. She led Blacky back to the castle.

"A holiday," said the Princess in Black. She crawled back up the secret chute.

"A holiday?" asked the Princess in Black. She shrugged into her frilly dress. She was no longer the Princess in Black.

"A holiday!" said Princess Magnolia.

The Goat Avenger would stay in the pasture. He would watch out for monsters and save the goats.

Princess Magnolia packed. The best time to start a holiday was right now.

Chapter 5

Princess Magnolia rode her bicycle to the seaside. After all, her pony deserved a holiday too.

The air was salty. The sun was shiny. The sea was as blue as monster fur. It was a perfect day.

Princess Magnolia lay down in a hammock. She closed her eyes. She was just about to snore when some-one said, "Hello, Princess Magnolia."

Princess Magnolia opened her eyes. Next to her was a pile of snacks. Beside the snacks was another hammock. On that hammock was a book. Behind the book was Princess Sneezewort.

"What a surprise!" said Princess Magnolia in her cheeriest sleepy voice.

"You sound tired," said Princess Sneezewort. "You should take a nap. I'll make sure no one wakes you."

"Thank you, Princess Sneezewort," said Princess Magnolia.

"Of course," she said. "That's what friends are for."

Princess Magnolia closed her eyes again.

"Later," Princess Sneezewort whispered, "we can play checkers."

Princess Magnolia was just about to snore again when she heard a noise.

"ROAR!"

Princess Magnolia kept her eyes shut. A monster? On the perfect beach? Impossible.

"ROARRR!"

Princess Magnolia squeezed her eyes shutter. Maybe she was already asleep. Maybe she was dreaming.

"ROAAARRRR!"

Princess Magnolia peeked with one eye.

A huge head rose out of the water. The head was on a long neck. The neck was attached to a massive body.

A sea monster was terrorizing her perfect beach.

"Sorry!" said Princess Sneezewort. "I didn't know how to make sure a sea monster didn't wake you."

And Princess Magnolia didn't know how to make sure a sea monster didn't hurt Princess Sneezewort.

Princess Magnolia wore glass flip-flops. Princess Magnolia sunburned easily. Second-storey windows made Princess Magnolia feel woozy.

Princess Magnolia could not fight a sea monster.

Chapter 6

The Goat Avenger stood tall in the goat pasture. Fists on hips. Chin raised. Smile sparkling. He waited for monsters to come.

The goats chewed some grass.

The Goat Avenger chopped at the air. He rolled on the grass. He said, "YAAA!"

The goats swallowed. Then they chewed some more grass.

The Goat Avenger tried out some catchphrases.

WATCH OUT!

SHOO!

One of the goats burped.

The Goat Avenger went over to the hole. Monster Land was down there. All week long monsters had been climbing out of that hole. The Goat Avenger had created his own monster alarm using ropes and bells. But nothing moved.

"Hello?" the Goat Avenger whispered. "Monsters?"

The goats chewed more grass.

Chapter 7

Maybe if I just lie here the monster will go away, thought Princess Magnolia.

"ROOOAAARRR!" said the sea monster. "EAT PEOPLE!"

The people on the beach screamed.

"People are screaming," said Princess Sneezewort.

People ran.

"People are running," said Princess Sneezewort. "Should we run too?"

People dropped ice lollies in the sand.

"That boy dropped his ice lolly in the sand," said Princess Sneezewort.

"EAT PEOPLE!" roared the sea monster. "PEOPLE YUM!"

Princess Magnolia sighed.

"You're right, Princess Sneezewort," she said. "We should run."

Some say that princesses don't run. But these two did. They ran very fast.

Princess Sneezewort ran towards an ice-cream stand. Princess Magnolia ran towards a bathing tent. She needed her disguise, and fast.

Nobody knew that prim and perfect Princess Magnolia was secretly the Princess in Black. But she had to keep the sea monster from eating people, especially Princess Sneezewort. After all, that's what friends are for.

Chapter 8

Duff the goat boy sat and watched the goats chew. His mask had itched. His cape had chafed. So he'd taken them off.

He wished he'd brought a book.

Clang-clang-clang.

"The monster alarm!" said Duff.

Duff shoved on his mask. He tied on his cape. He was no longer Duff the goat boy.

The Goat Avenger put his fists on his hips and said, "Ha-ha!"

Nothing came out of the hole.

The rope on the monster alarm was wiggling. The goat bells were clanging. But there was no monster in sight.

Chapter 9

The Princess in Black stood on the beach. She said, "Sea monster, you may not eat people."

"ROARRR!" said the sea monster. Its tail slapped the water. A wave crashed to shore.

Maybe it can't hear me, she thought.

The Princess in Black climbed onto a rock. She cupped her hands around her mouth.

She said, "Behave, beast!"

"ROAARRRR!" said the sea monster. Its tail whipped the beach. It barely missed the ice-cream stand.

Maybe it still can't hear me, she thought.

She leapt onto its tail. She started to run up. Suddenly the tail lifted into the air.

The Princess in Black slipped. Then she slipped some more. She grabbed the tail and hugged it tight.

Don't look down, she told herself.

She looked down. She gasped. The bathing tents looked like pebbles. The people looked like ants.

A bird landed on her shoulder.

"Squawk?" said the Princess in Black. That meant "Could you fly me down?"

"Squawk, squawk," said the bird. That meant "So sorry, but you're too heavy."

"Squawk..." said the Princess in Black. That meant "This was supposed to be a holiday..."

Chapter 10

The Goat Avenger squinted into the hole. Not so much as a tentacle appeared.

Then what was setting off the monster alarm?

A mystery! The Goat Avenger straightened his mask. He tightened his cape (a little too tight). He loosened his cape. Then he followed the rope back to a tree.

A furry creature was caught in the rope. It was flailing! It was squeaking! It was ... a squirrel.

CLANG!

CLANG!

"At last! A monster!" said the Goat Avenger.

A nearby goat bleated doubtfully.

"A squirrel could be a monster," the Goat Avenger explained to the doubtful goat. "If you're an acorn."

The Goat Avenger freed the squirrel.

He said, "Don't eat any goats."

The squirrel squeaked. It ran away. Off to find acorns to terrorize.

The goats said, "Maaaa." That probably meant that they were proud of the Goat Avenger.

But the Goat Avenger shrugged. He'd had his heart set on a real monster. A scary monster.

Chapter 11

The sea monster's tail was long, narrow and slick. It reminded the Princess in Black of her secret chute. That gave her an idea.

SWOOP!

If she hadn't been so tired, the
sliding would have been a lot of fun.

The sea monster's back was soft and springy, like her mattress. She had to jump to get across it.

If she hadn't been so tired, the jumping would have been a lot of fun.

The sea monster's neck was as high as a tower. She had to climb to get up.

Actually, even though she was tired, the climbing was a lot of fun.

She wondered about getting a sea monster for a pet. But it would never fit in her moat.

At last she reached its head. The sea monster tried to bat her off. So the Princess in Black and the sea monster waged battle.

She skimmed down to the tip of its nose. She looked it square in the eyes.

"EAT PEOPLE!" said the sea monster.

"No!" said the Princess in Black. "You may not eat people!"

The sea monster could hear her now. It frowned.

"NO?"

"No," she said.

The sea monster sniffled. Its neck drooped. Its tail sagged.

"Um ... you could eat fish," said the Princess in Black.

The sea monster straightened up.

"YES!" it said. "EAT FISH!"

The monster dove back into the sea. The Princess in Black had no choice but to follow.

Chapter 12

The Goat Avenger swung in a hammock. He sipped lemonade. He read a comic book.

The squirrel hopped onto his shoulder. The Goat Avenger shared his lemonade. It was a good day.

Clang-clang-clang.

"Probably another squirrel," said the Goat Avenger.

He stood and turned around.

An acorn-shaped monster with one huge eye lurked beside the hole.

"AAAH!" said the Goat Avenger.

"ROAR!" said the acorn-shaped monster.

"SQUIRREL!" said the Goat Avenger. "Terrorize that acorn!"

"SQUEAK!" said the squirrel.

"AAAAHH!" said the acorn-shaped monster. It leapt back into the hole.

The Goat Avenger put his fists on his hips. He had done it! After all, he had saved the squirrel. And the squirrel had scared away the monster. Thanks to him, the goats were safe. And somewhere, thanks to him, the Princess in Black was having a holiday.

Chapter 13

The sea monster plunged into the water. The ocean rose up. A wave formed. And the Princess in Black was on top of it.

The water washed away her disguise. The wave rolled her to an island. It dumped her on the shore.

Princess Magnolia looked around. The island was tiny. Nothing for miles. No screaming people. No ear-licking goats. And no monsters.

It was perfect.

Princess Magnolia curled up in the shade of the coconut tree.

"Holiday," she said.

She closed her eyes. She said "Snore." And then she did just that.

FLY, BLACKY, FLY!

More adventures with the Princess in Black...

SHANNON & DEAN HALE are the husband-and-wife writing team behind the graphic novels *Rapunzel's Revenge* and *Calamity Jack*, both illustrated by Nathan Hale. Shannon Hale is also the author of the Newbery Honor-winning novel *Princess Academy*, the *New York Times* bestselling Ever After High series, and others. About this book, they say, "Sometimes our daughters wear princess dresses and play tea party, and sometimes they don capes and fight monsters. We wanted to write a character who does both, too!" Shannon and Dean Hale live in Salt Lake City, Utah, with their four young children.

LeUYEN PHAM is the illustrator of many books for children, including *God's Dream* by Archbishop Desmond Tutu and *Aunt Mary's Rose* by Douglas Wood. About this book, she says, "I was never a very princessy girl, and I always preferred playing superheroes to playing girl games. I would have *loved* this book as a kid!" LeUyen Pham lives in California with her husband, who is also an artist, and their two small boys, who are superheroes by day and mini-monsters by night.